GRANDPA'S SLIPPERS

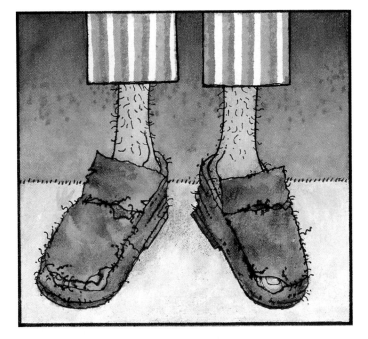

by Joy Watson

Illustrated by Wendy Hodder

READ BY READING

Ashton Scholastic

Auckland Sydney New York Toronto London

On Monday,
Grandma looked at Grandpa's old slippers.
"You need new slippers," she said.
"Those are going to fall to bits."

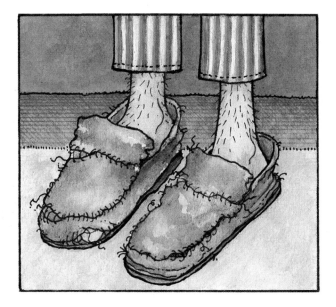

"Nonsense," said Grandpa.
"My slippers are fine."

"But they have holes in their soles,"
said Grandma.

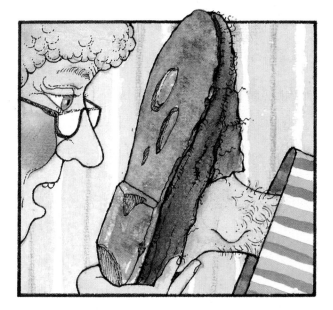

"Good," said Grandpa.
"That's how I like them."

Nevertheless,
Grandma bought him a new pair of slippers
that day.
Grandpa refused to wear them.

On Tuesday,
Grandpa was cleaning out
the cupboard under the stairs
when he came upon his old slippers
hidden away in the darkest corner.

"Leave my slippers alone," he told Grandma.
"Don't try to hide them!"

"They should be hidden," said Grandma.
"They're going to fall to bits.
They have holes in their soles
and the stitching has come undone."

"Good," said Grandpa.
"That's how I like them."

On Wednesday,
Grandpa was just in time
to see Grandma handing his old slippers
to a person collecting used clothing.

"Hey! Leave my slippers alone," he told Grandma.
"Don't try to give them away!"

"They should be given away," said Grandma.
"They're going to fall to bits.
They have holes in their soles,
the stitching has come undone
and all the fluff has worn off."

"Good," said Grandpa.
"That's how I like them."

On Thursday,
Grandpa went to check
if the rubbish bag had been put out.
There, right on the top, were his old slippers.

"Do leave my slippers alone,"
he told Grandma.
"Don't try to throw them away."

"They should be thrown away," said Grandma.
"They're going to fall to bits.
They have holes in their soles,
the stitching has come undone,
all the fluff has worn off
and I can see your toes."

"Good," said Grandpa.
"That's how I like them."

On Friday,
Grandpa took some potato peelings
out to the compost heap.
There, not quite covered by a cabbage leaf,
were his old slippers.

"Please leave my slippers alone,"
he told Grandma.
"Don't try to bury them in the compost heap!"

"They should be buried," said Grandma.
"They're going to fall to bits.
They have holes in their soles,
the stitching has come undone,
all the fluff has worn off
and I can see your toes.
They're *so* tatty."

"Good," said Grandpa.
"That's how I like them."

On Saturday,
Grandpa was just about to set fire
to a pile of leaves in the garden
when a sudden gust of wind revealed —
his old slippers!

"Oh, no!" said Grandpa, and he told Grandma,
"Once and for all,
will you please leave my old slippers alone.
Don't try to burn them."

"Very well, but they should be burned,"
said Grandma.
"They're going to fall to bits.
They have holes in their soles,
the stitching has come undone,
all the fluff has worn off
and I can see your toes.
They're *so* tatty
and they look very uncomfortable."

"Good," said Grandpa.
"That's how I like them."

On Sunday morning,
Grandpa got out of bed
and was about to put on his old slippers
when they fell to bits in his hands!

He had to wear his new slippers instead.
They had whole soles, strong stitching,
warm fluff covering his toes
and they looked neat and natty.

Grandpa was surprised to find
that they were actually very comfortable indeed.

He was very pleased and so was Grandma.

On Monday,
Grandma looked at Grandpa's old grey cardigan.
"You need a new cardigan," she said.